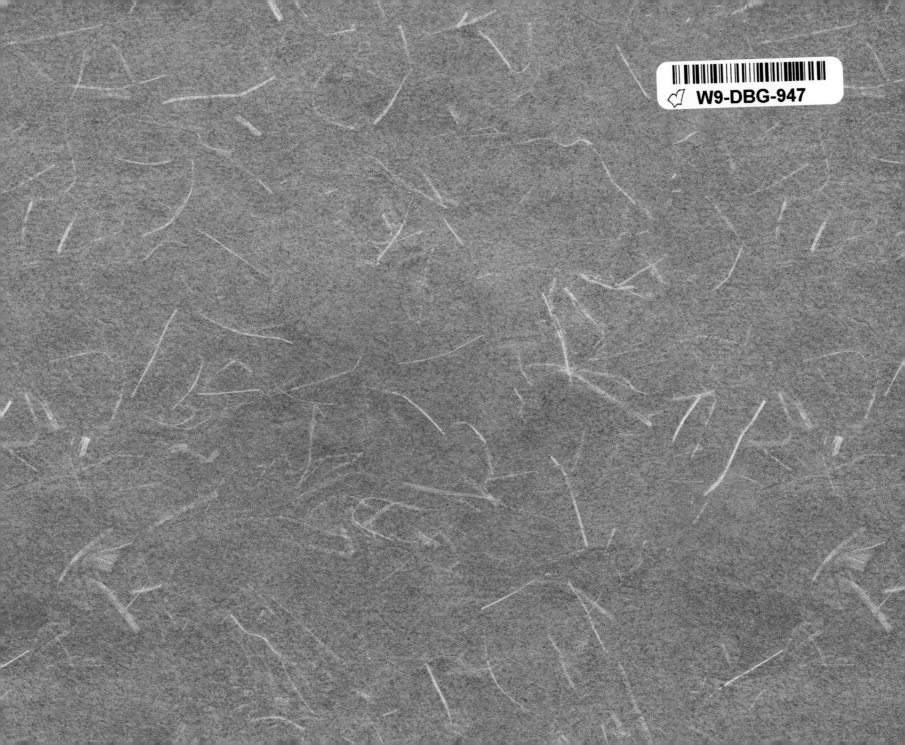

Library of Congress
Cataloging-in-Publication Data available.

ISBN: 978-1-68555-004-2

Ebook ISBN: 978-1-68555-005-9

LCCN: 2021951823

Printed using Forest Stewardship Council certified
stock from sustainably managed forests.

Manufactured in China.

Design by Elliot Kreloff.

2 4 6 8 10 9 7 5 3 1

The Collective Book Studio®
Oakland, California
www.thecollectivebook.studio

Once upon a line

elliot kreloff

THE
collective
BOOK STUDIO

Once upon a time, a line was drawn.

Line was excited to be a line,
but he wondered . . .

Hey everybody, look at me. I'M A LINE!

What does a line do?

Line asked his mom and his dad.

So, Line tried going straight . . .

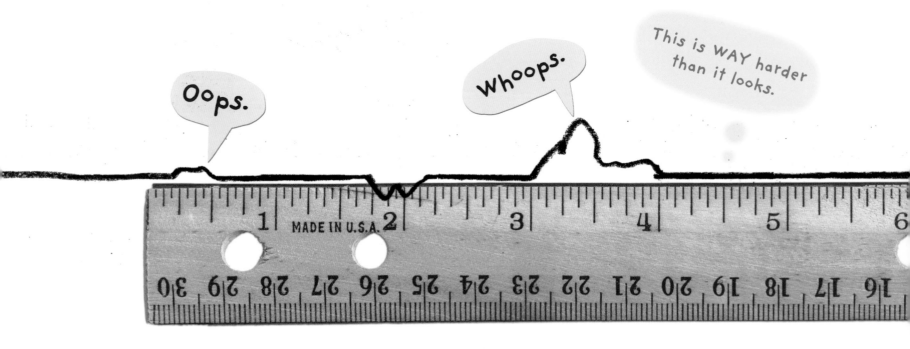

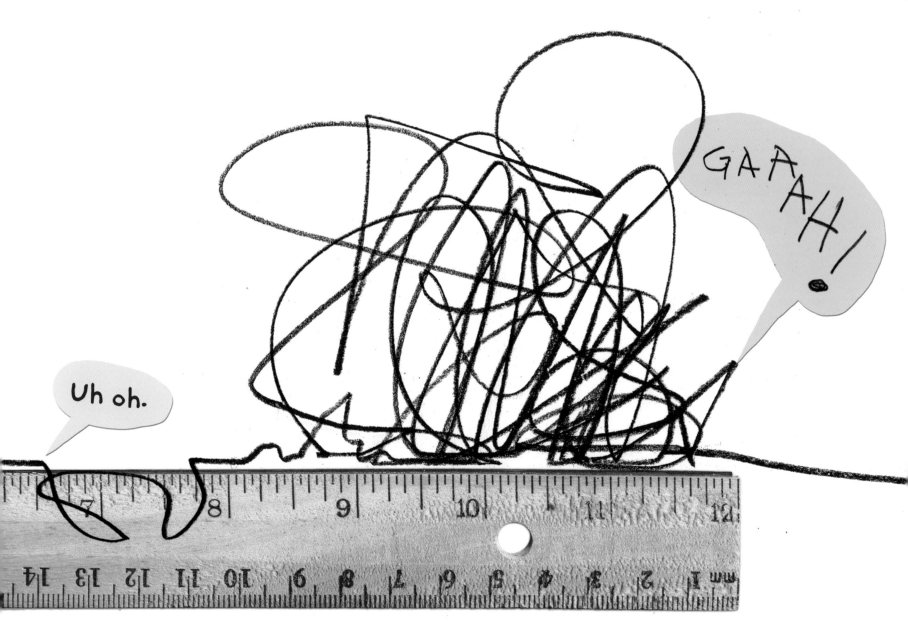

. . . but it didn't feel right.

Line asked his friends.

Square and Rectangle knew all about corners.

We call that doing the box step.

They told Line to try turning some on his own.

But I'm back where I started.

TURN, baby! TURN!

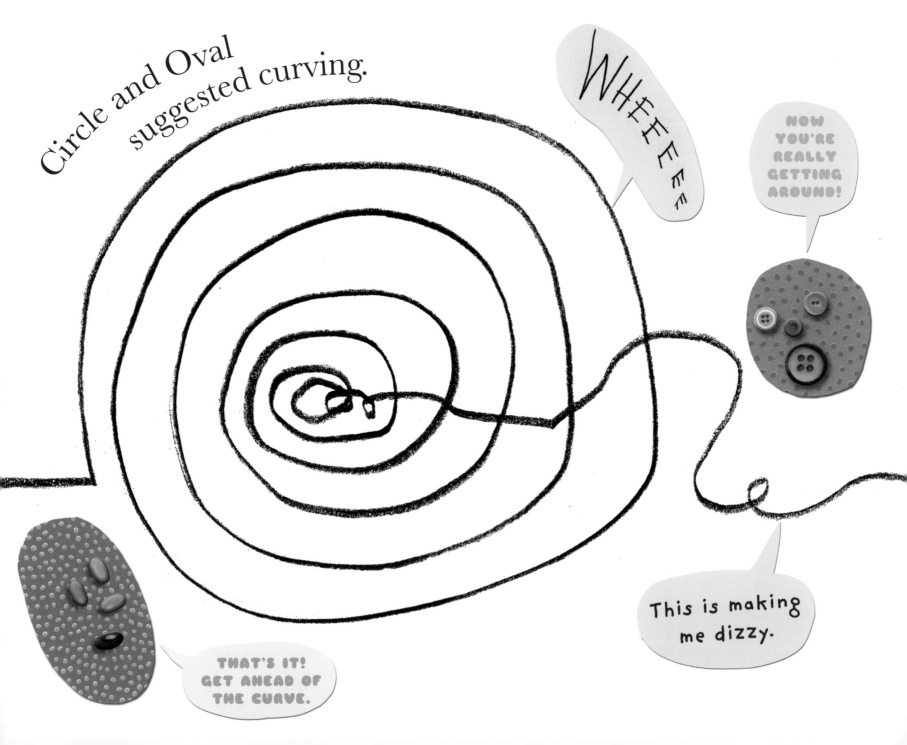

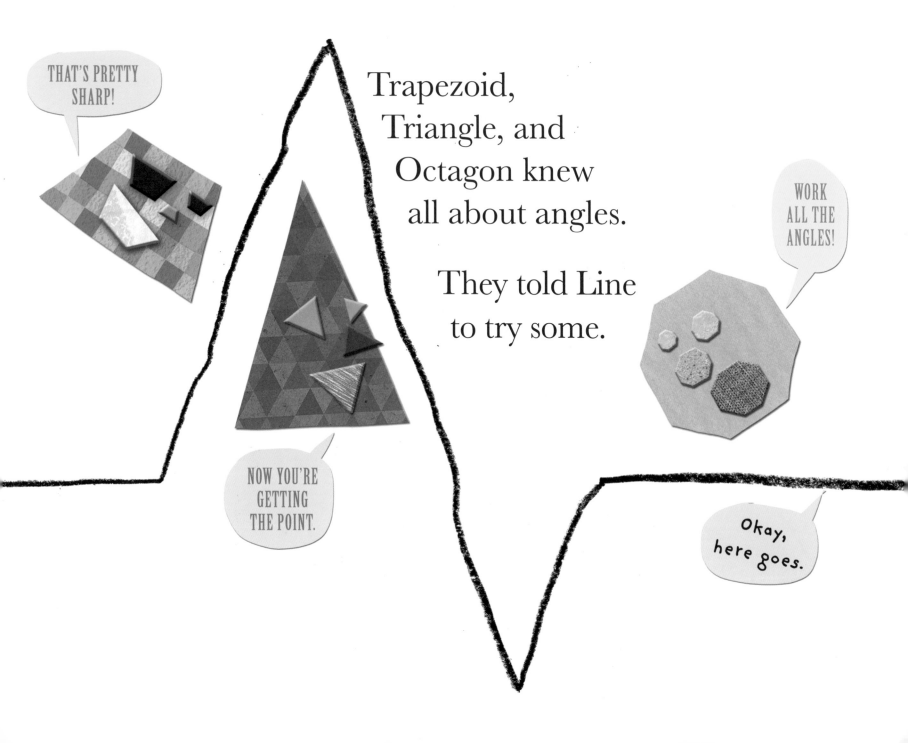

Trapezoid, Triangle, and Octagon knew all about angles.

They told Line to try some.

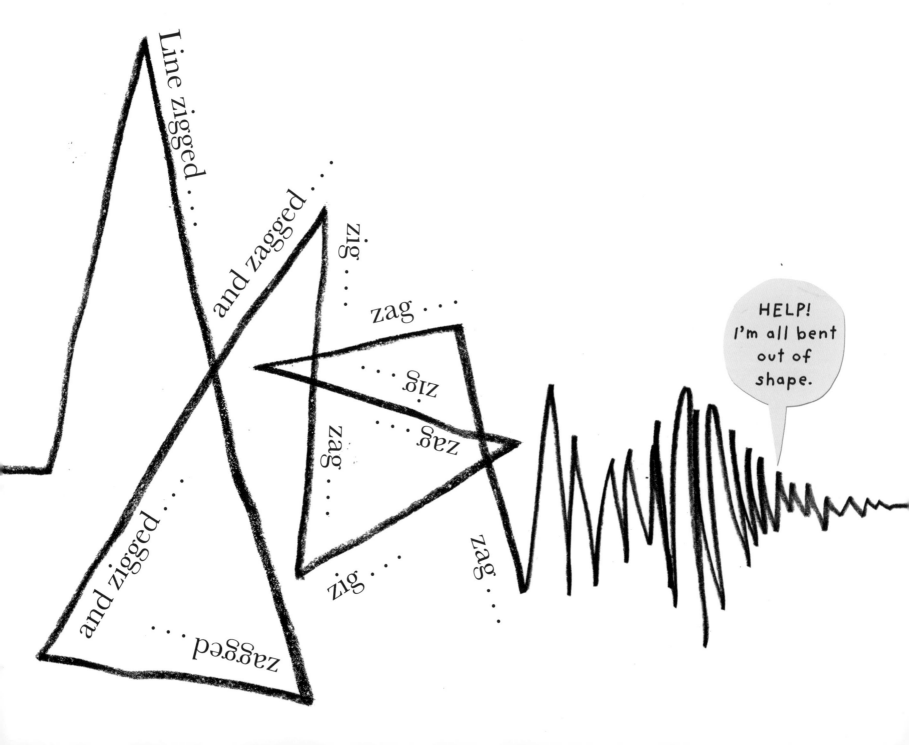

Line still didn't know his purpose.
He decided he needed to get out in the world and
broaden his horizon.

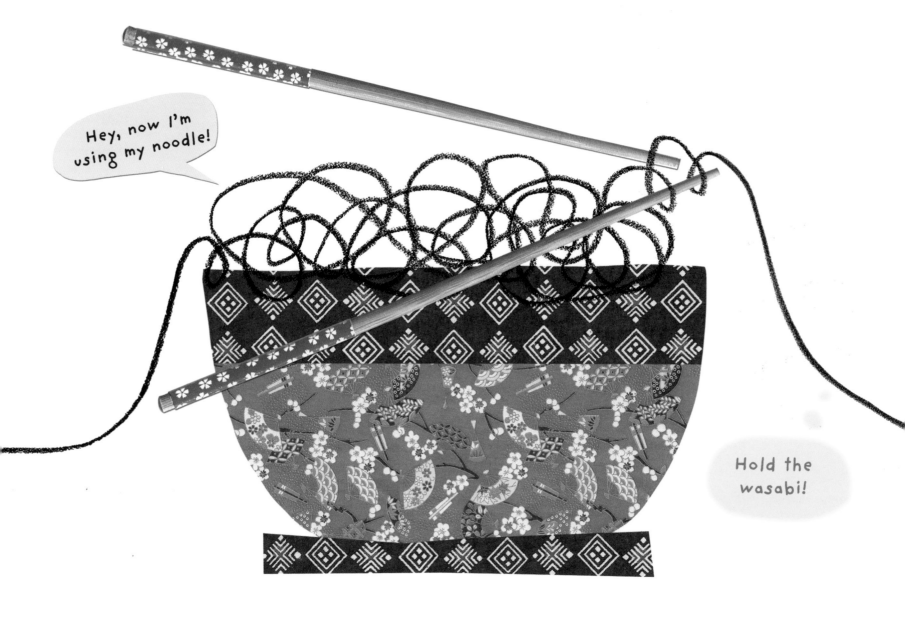

Line went east. Very, very far east.   Too spicy!

Line went west.   Too wild.

Line went north.   Too cold.

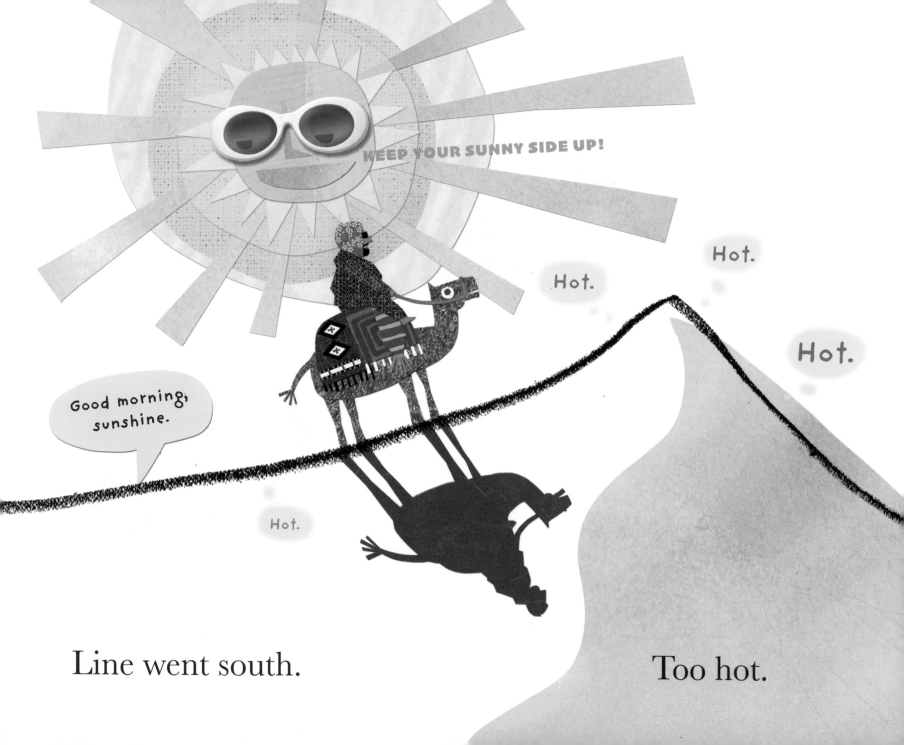

Line went farther south.   Way too cold.

Line took to the open sea.　　　　He got seasick.

Line tried joining a circus.

Too much pressure.

Line tried joining a rock band.   Too, too LOUD.

Line took to the sky.

Up, up, up Line went . . .

Wherever Line went,
and whatever Line tried,
Line still had not
discovered his purpose.

Line went home, where everyone wanted to hear about Line's adventures.

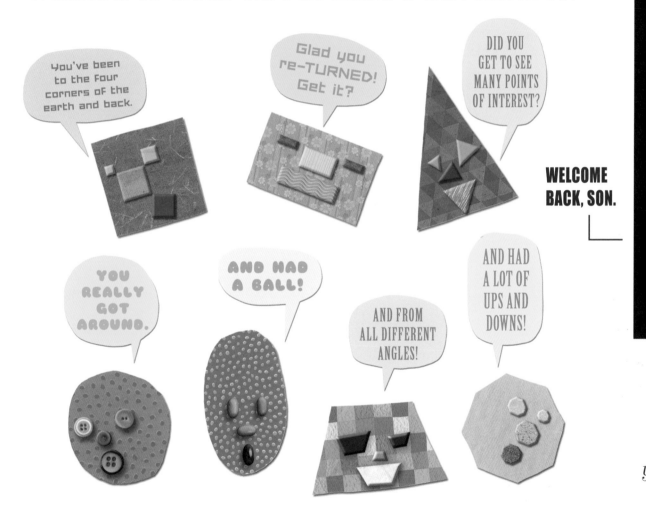

You've been to the four corners of the earth and back.

Glad you re-TURNED! Get it?

DID YOU GET TO SEE MANY POINTS OF INTEREST?

YOU REALLY GOT AROUND.

AND HAD A BALL!

AND FROM ALL DIFFERENT ANGLES!

AND HAD A LOT OF UPS AND DOWNS!

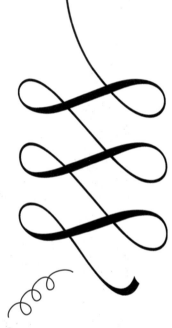

WELCOME BACK, SON.

Well dear, did you feel that you left your mark on the world?

No. Not really.

Then Line had a really BIG idea.

Line didn't need someone else to give him a purpose.

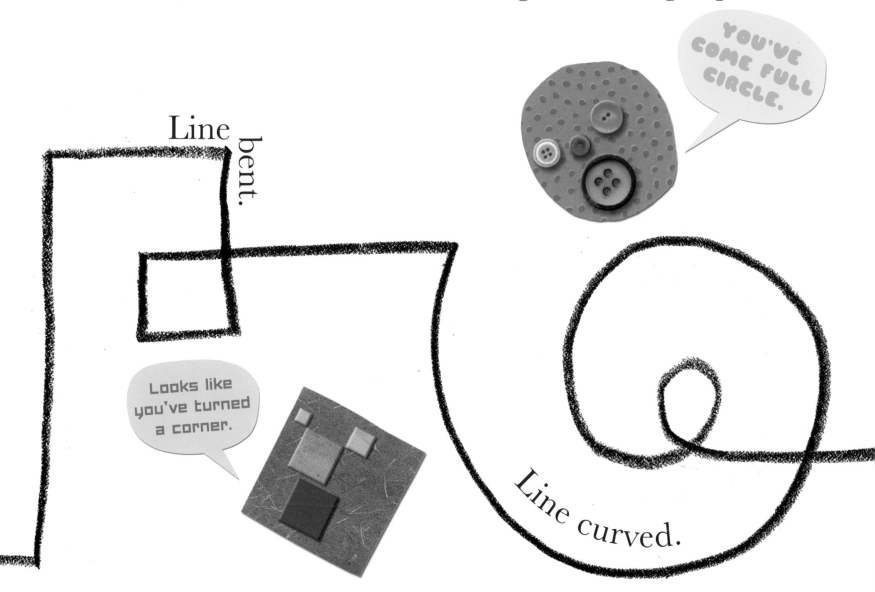

Line used all the things he learned from his travels and from his friends.

Then Line had an even **BIGGER** idea.

with many thanks to Saul Steinberg

When I was growing up, my parents subscribed to a magazine called *The New Yorker*. Every issue had cartoons. My favorites were those by Saul Steinberg.

A few years ago, I was lucky enough to see a 33-foot-long drawing of his called *The Line*, on display at the Morgan Library. The drawing starts with a hand holding a pen drawing a line, with a face floating above it. As the line travels across the 33 feet of paper, it becomes the edge of the water in Venice, a clothesline, a train trestle, a bridge, a desk—on and on until it ends where it started as a line drawn by a hand holding a pen. You can see an animated version of this drawing online at: https://youtu.be/n4PKZhdx_MY

As I looked at Mr. Steinberg's line, I wondered: What if that line could talk? What would the line think as he traveled around the world, turning into different things? Why did the line decide to take the trip? This book is my way to honor and thank Mr. Steinberg for all the wonderful drawings he gave us, and for helping me, when I was a boy, to take up the pencil and "find my purpose."

—Elliot Kreloff

You can find out all about Saul Steinberg and see his artwork at the website of The Saul Steinberg Foundation: https://saulsteinbergfoundation.org